Forcibly B

Kate Pullinger

A Phoenix Paperback

Forcibly Bewitched first published in *New Woman Magazine* in 1994.
*Franz Kafka's Shirt, The Wardrobe, The Battersea Power Station,
Lois and The Ancients, The Unbearable Shortness of Holidays,
The Fact-Finding Mission* published in *Tiny Lies*
by Cape/Picador, 1988

This edition published in 1996 by Phoenix
a division of Orion Books Ltd
Orion House, 5 Upper St Martin's Lane, London WC2H 9EA

ISBN 1 85799 755 7

Typeset by Deltatype Ltd, Ellesmere Port, Cheshire
Printed in Great Britain by Clays Ltd, St Ives plc

Contents

Forcibly Bewitched

Lois stood behind a woman whose grey-blonde hair was cut in a perfect line across her neck, like a bleached Louise Brooks. They were both attempting to look at a painting on the wall, but were stuck behind another woman pushing an elderly man in a wheelchair. The family resemblance between the pusher and the pushed was remarkable; Lois had noticed the pair earlier when someone else behind whom she had been standing whispered, 'Isn't that Sir Harold Arnold?' The gallery was very crowded. In a moment the wheelchair would roll on to the next painting, the blonde Louise Brooks (it was dyed, it had to be – now that Lois had started dyeing her hair she took pleasure in assuming that everyone else did too) would have a look and then Lois could take her turn to gaze at the painting, at the two-hundred-year-old blobs of oil and egg-wash or whatever it was that painters used to fix the canvas back then.

There was a man following Lois, she was almost sure of it, although he might be following Louise Brooks; in fact, come to think of it, Lois was following Louise, everybody was following everybody else around the concourse of the gallery. Lois looked forward to the day she could view the paintings on CD-Rom InterNet E-Mail and would no longer have to visit museums and galleries in person. No, it wasn't true, she liked the crush of popular shows. Her mother had always seen picture-viewing as a chance for 'a bit of a stroll'; she was an eternal dieter and relished the opportunity to do two things at once: culture and exercise, hence a brisk walk around a large museum before tea and cakes. Lois saw the insides of a lot of museums when she was a child, but she had never been allowed to linger over the antiquities, so now when she went to exhibitions she proceeded very slowly and sat a lot, gazing at the paintings, stepping up close to peer at the brush work. Francisco Goya painted that with his own hands, she found herself thinking today, he himself stepped up to the easel on his short legs and applied his brush to the canvas. Painting seemed a physical art; Lois wished she was an artist instead of working in an office, but she knew that was like wishing she had been an astronaut.

Sir Harold Arnold's daughter pushed her father's wheelchair onward and Louise Brooks shuffled ahead and Lois took a step too, then stopped, and the person behind her trod on the back of her heel. Lois hated when that happened. She turned to see who had done it. It was him, the man who had been following her. He was short, he had longish curly black hair, and he smiled up at her rather uncertainly after murmuring an apology. 'Let's get out of here,' he said, taking a step backward into the middle of the room, the space suddenly, miraculously, clear. He reached out and took her hand and took another step backward, drawing her with him, and for a moment Lois thought he was going to burst into a song. She held her breath. Was this how it felt to be in a musical? She waited.

But he did not sing. He dropped Lois's hand and said 'Only joking.' Lois frowned and turned to discover she had lost her place in the crowd snaking round the walls of the gallery. She turned back to admonish Mr Friendly but, of course, he had gone.

Lois managed to insert her body into a gap in the queue and she viewed the rest of the exhibition happily. She had slipped away from the office early; if her boss mentioned it tomorrow she had only to tell him where she had been and, impressed by her edification, he would not mention it again. He was like her father that way, easily over-awed by culture, ashamed of his own ignorance. Lois's father had never accompanied his wife and daughter on their jogs around museums; just as well, thought Lois now, gives me something to do if he ends up in a wheelchair.

Lois had married at twenty-two, divorced at twenty-eight, and now, at thirty-two, found herself ensconced in a dwarfish spinsterhood which she rather enjoyed. She had a nice flat, a good job, friends, and she lived near Sainsbury's. Movies, books, a little theatre, restaurants, shopping, cooking, the odd holiday – a lot of flavour, but no spice, as her mother was fond of saying. Lois did not care what her mother thought, and her mother knew it; the disapproved of marriage, then the unheard of, unmentionable, divorce had ensured that. Lois liked the way her life had turned out; being on her own had not made her unhappy. However, she was not altogether sanguine about the lack of spice.

When Lois emerged blinking from the gallery into the summer haze of pollen and pollution, her man sat waiting in the forecourt of the gallery. His little legs were crossed and he grasped his knee with both hands as he watched Lois come down the steps towards him. His hair seemed even curlier in the humidity. Lois sat beside him.

'I thought you were going to sing in there,' she said.

'So did I, but it seemed inappropriate somehow,' he replied.

Lois found herself agreeing to go have coffee and, as they walked in companionable silence – it was too hot to speak – she found herself thinking that she had never done this before, accepted an invitation from a complete stranger. But then she corrected herself – I can be so deluded sometimes – because the truth was she did this kind of thing all the time.

There had been that man she met on a bus, she had gone for a drink with him; his eyes were so blue. He was Polish and once he had told her that he might as well have given up there and then because Lois could not stop thinking about the word Polish and was it really spelt just like polish and how unfortunate. Then there had been that Nigerian man who had turned out to be very rich; Lois had gone out to dinner with him, but they had disagreed about politics. Lois

could be shockingly left-wing – she shocked herself sometimes – and he had turned out to be amazingly right-wing.
She let him pay for dinner. And there had been that man she
met in a bookshop when they both reached for the only
copy of *Pride and Prejudice*. But she had married him: never
trust a man who reads Jane Austen was the lesson she
learned from that. One of the lessons.

'Do you read Austen?' she asked the short man who
walked beside her now.

'Auster?' he asked, but just then they came to a busy
road; their destination was on the opposite side. He took
her by the hand once again. His hand was smaller than hers,
cool and dry, which was commendable given the heat. I like
a man with cool, dry hands, she thought, and then they
made their dash, his five foot six frame sure-footed next to
her five foot ten.

Lois's mother had a thing about men and height; the only
good men were tall. Lois's father was six foot seven, which
even now seemed a little extreme. When Lois was young she
had fallen for her mother's height fetish and the man she
married was a decent six foot three. But it turned out to be a
disastrous misconception, one of many of which her
mother was fond, like only married women can use
tampons and only widowed women wear black. Life was
just not like that anymore.

The coffee house was busy but they found a table near the
back. 'Did you see the painting?' he asked.

'Which one?'

' "Forcibly Bewitched".'

Lois recalled it; a priest with mad, rolling eyes was lighting an oil lamp held by the devil, a grey, horned satyr, while donkeys danced upright on their hind feet in the background. It was one of a group of paintings of flying witches, cannibals, and lunatic asylums, the kind of thing for which she appreciated Goya.

'Yes, I saw it.'

He nodded, he seemed satisfied.

'You are an incredible beauty,' he said.

Now this was something new to Lois. No man with whom she had gone off had ever said anything like that to her before. She nodded, but did not reply. What did he mean by 'incredible'? Did he mean strange? Did he mean surprising, as in not to be believed, as in weird? Did using the words incredible and beauty together actually cancel them both out leaving only ugliness in their stead? Lois thought about this while she looked at her short, curly-haired companion.

'I meant incomparable,' he said.

'Oh,' replied Lois, 'well, that's all right then.'

Their courtship took place quickly. Lois found herself entirely enamoured. His name was Beverley and she was enchanted by the idea of having a boyfriend with a girl's name, as if that might mean he would have fewer of the foibles of previous lovers, more of the charms of a good friend. She loved to tower over him in public and he seemed to enjoy it as well; it became a kind of secret joke between them, creating a *frisson* Lois imagined somehow akin to S&M. It felt kinky, that was all. She was excited by it.

They began spending all their free time together. They went to every exhibition in the city that summer, the more crowded the better. Bev would follow directly behind Lois and, in the crush of beholding great art, Lois would feel Bev's body pressed to hers, her buttocks level with his abdomen. She would find herself blushing and, when there was room, she would turn to face him and he would smile at her silkily. Once, just once, he actually did sing. It was an aria from an opera they had recently attended; the lover dies and as she dies, she sings. Bev kept his voice low, he held both of Lois's hands, she caught and held his words even though they were Italian. None of the other exhibition-goers seemed to notice what was happening. It was as though Beverley and Lois were in a higher place.

Franz Kafka's Shirt

Genevieve paid a great deal of attention to her dreams because she believed they revealed important things about her state of mind. Her dream-life was particularly rich; Genevieve could often remember her dreams with a clarity that she rarely found in her actual waking life. Her dreams were like little absurdist plays, one after the other, night after night. It was as if Ionesco had moved into her subconscious.

From time to time Genevieve's dreams were more straightforward, tiny snippets of wish-fulfilment that lasted five seconds, like the night she dreamed she was given a pen, the ink of which would never blot, and the time she went back to school and humiliated the boy who once told her she was ugly. But, more often her dreams made little obvious sense and Genevieve had to spend whole mornings figuring out what they meant. She had her own set of dream-analysis tools, and her own ideas about the symbolism within her. Not for her the Freudian, Jungian, Reichian interpretations, nor even the more hippy ideas of dreaming and astrology.

Genevieve's dreams were like theatre, so she interpreted

them like theatre. She enjoyed them and queued for ice-cream in the interval. She appreciated the art behind their creation, and she admired the design of the sets. Most of all, she was thrilled with the way she almost always knew all the people in the dream. It was like having a fringe theatre company devoted to the interpretation of one's own life. That was how Genevieve saw her dreams: very interesting, often disturbing, but something that didn't actually have much impact upon the everyday occurrences of her diurnal life.

In this waking life, Genevieve was a normalish type of person. She had a job she didn't like, although it didn't annoy her enough to make her look for another one. She had a pleasant social life and spent many happy evenings arguing with her friends in front of the fire. She went to the cinema, the theatre, the odd party, she wore lipstick in the evening, and she smoked too much. She fell in love and had her heart broken. And she had vivid dreams every night. Genevieve didn't feel there was anything particularly lacking from her own life, although many of her friends, with lives just like hers, did.

Occasionally Genevieve and her friends talked about their dreams. When Genevieve told the others about hers everybody laughed and said they wished they had such entertaining, strange, nonsensical dreams. No one thought there could possibly be anything wrong with the way Genevieve was dreaming.

One night Genevieve dreamed she was wearing Franz

Kafka's shirt. In this very brief dream all that happened was Genevieve found herself standing on the pavement in front of where she lived. She looked down at what she was wearing and when she saw the shirt she had on, she knew that it was Franz Kafka's shirt. That was it. That was all that happened in the dream.

But the weekend after having that dream, and after Genevieve and her friends had had a good giggle at the absurdity of it, Genevieve went to a jumble sale. As she was looking through a pile of shirts on a table in the church hall she found herself holding a shirt that she felt, against all probability, was Franz Kafka's shirt. It was an ordinary man's shirt of a variety often to be found at jumble sales, cotton-mix, rather soiled around the collar, and worn thin on the left elbow. The only remarkable thing about this shirt, other than the fact that Genevieve was sure it was Franz Kafka's shirt, was that it was printed with a motif of beige cowboys on beige bucking broncos. It was a discreet motif, the sort of print one would not notice unless one really looked at that kind of thing, like someone with a theory about understanding men by examining the patterns on their shirts. Genevieve was not that kind of person.

Quickly, and not without exhibiting embarrassment, Genevieve bought the shirt from the elderly woman behind the table insisting on paying twenty pence instead of the ten pence for which the woman had asked. She took the shirt home with her and soaked it in the bath tub for the afternoon, hoping to remove the stain around the neck, and also, even if she didn't think of it, hoping to remove whatever it was about the shirt that made her think it was Franz Kafka's. While it soaked Genevieve sat in the kitchen. She told herself that Franz Kafka had been dead for rather a long time, and as far as she knew he had never lived in her neighbourhood, let alone her country, and the chances that a shirt that had been anywhere near Franz Kafka would turn up at a jumble sale in South London were very slim. As well as all that, she felt quite certain having read several of his books that Franz Kafka would not have worn a shirt with a motif of cowboys on bucking broncos adorning it, no matter how discreet.

Still, once she had taken the shirt out of the tub, washed it, wrung it dry, and hung it up, and then looked at it hanging there, rather limp and not even terribly stylish, she knew that it was Franz Kafka's shirt and there was nothing she could do about it.

So, she wore it. She wore it to parties, she wore it to work, she wore it to the cinema. No one ever noticed the shirt, except for a few people who laughed at the cowboys, and although Genevieve lived with the hope that one day someone would say 'Hey! Isn't that Franz Kafka's shirt?' no one ever did. Gradually Genevieve became accustomed to wearing Franz Kafka's shirt and the urge to find someone to talk to about it, an urge that came over her with particular strength when she was drunk, faded. All she was left with was a rather uninteresting looking piece of clothing, and a faint sense that something, somewhere, was odd.

Genevieve's life went on as it always had done and her dream-life continued as well. More miniature absurdist dramas took place in her mind than at any real theatre. These dreams continued to amuse Genevieve, and her friends.

Then, one night during the wet and bleak London winter, months after she had dreamed about Franz Kafka's shirt, Genevieve dreamed about swimming. She was swimming with Franz Kafka in a murky, muddy river. Franz Kafka was wearing a swimming costume, modern and brief in style, printed with the same pattern as his shirt, cowboys and bucking broncos. They were swimming the Australian crawl side by side when Franz Kafka suddenly stopped and shouted at Genevieve, 'What makes you think you can wear a dead writer's clothes?' Genevieve also stopped swimming and turned her body in the water so she could face him. 'That was my favourite shirt,' he added indignantly.

'Oh, was it?' said Genevieve. 'Don't you think you've been dead for rather too long to be complaining about this sort of thing?'

'Humph,' said Franz Kafka, cheekily, 'I suppose it will be my shoes next. Or, perhaps, Dostoevsky's underwear, eh?'

'Shut up,' Genevieve shouted, 'you're dead!' And with that, she lunged at Franz Kafka, travelling through the water like a torpedo, and grabbed him around the neck. With one hand she attempted to throttle him whilst with the other she tried to twist off his head. The expression on Franz Kafka's face was terrible.

Genevieve woke up when she felt hot water on her hands. At first she thought it was Franz Kafka's blood, streaming from his neck, but she realised quickly that she had unscrewed her hot water bottle whilst dreaming. She screwed the top back in and then sat up, dismayed to find a colossal wet patch in the centre of the bed, like the unpleasant leftover of a wild sexual tryst.

Genevieve did not sleep for the remainder of the night and she was not to sleep for the many nights that followed. Early in the morning she would rise, put on Franz Kafka's shirt and go for long walks along the Thames. From Vauxhall Bridge she would stare down into the murky, muddy water of the river. She half expected to one day see the body of Franz Kafka floating there, identifiable by his swimming costume, the faint pattern of beige cowboys on beige bucking broncos.

The Wardrobe

After her sister went mad, Josephine couldn't see the point in carrying on behaving normally but she tried not to think about this and went on with her life. She herself had very little propensity towards madness; she had always been the practical one in the family. It was Fin, her sister, who'd been the flighty one. So when Fin went mad, or rather, decided to stop pretending and do what she wanted, it was Josephine who bore the brunt of it. It was she who made all the arrangements, it was she who consoled the rest of the family, and it was she who put on the brave face to the authorities. Everyone, including her brother Arthur, was incapacitated.

What Fin did is something that many people toy with doing, or perhaps are afraid they'll do. She began by leaving her phone off the hook for days on end, claiming that the noise it made when it rang frightened her and she was sure it would bring bad news. She stopped reading newspapers, listening to the radio and watching television. Talking to her became difficult.

One morning Fin wore her pyjamas to work. Her boss sent her home in a taxi. Fin went back to bed but got up again later in the day and, still in her pyjamas, went for a walk along the river. No one is exactly sure what happened next but Fin was spotted on Lambeth Bridge at about 6.00 p.m., walking along in her nightclothes which couldn't have afforded much protection against the elements. Half an hour later she was seen in an inner-tube floating past the Tower of London. When the police boat caught up with her she told them to leave her alone, she had decided to take to the high seas.

'I'm fucking fed up with all this shit,' she said to the police officer who was frightened by the look in her eyes. 'I'm fed up and I'm damn well getting away from this place. Look at that,' she shouted, pointing in the direction of the City. 'It's fucking disgusting, all those goddamn banks, there is no morality anyway, no one gives a damn about anything. I don't trust anyone anymore. You're all bloody liars. The whole world is one big fucking Masonic Lodge, I know it.' The police officer held on to Fin's arm, leaning over the edge of the boat. He listened to her carefully so that he could make a report. In the end all he wrote on his notepad was 'She's a nutter'. Fin was condemned but she didn't care one bit.

A little while later after Fin was picked up Josephine received a phone call from the police.

'Are you Josephine Cutler?' a male voice asked.

'Why, who are you?' Josephine replied.

'This is Sergeant Bulk speaking from the Metropolitan River Police. We've got a woman here who claims to be your sister. She identifies herself as Fin Cutler.'

'Yes, Fin is my sister,' said Josephine, feeling she already knew what had happened. 'I'll be right there.'

At the police station an officer led Josephine into the cells. Fin looked thin and tired as she shivered inside her blanket.

'Josephine!' she said. 'Tell them I do this all the time. Make them let me go, Josie. What bastards they are.'

'Fin, sweetheart, what happened?'

'I was trying to escape, babyface. I was trying to get out of this hellhole before it was too late. I know, I know,' she said shaking her head, 'I should have taken you and Arthur with me. But there just wasn't enough room and I had to get away. I wore my pyjamas so that no one could see me.'

'But, Fin, you can't get anywhere in an inner-tube on the Thames.'

'I could have Josie, if they'd given me a chance.'

A police officer cut Josephine's visit short so they could take her sister to the hospital. Over the next couple of weeks Fin told so many different stories that nobody wanted to listen to her any longer except Josephine and Arthur, but they didn't get to see her very often. Soon it was evident that Fin would have to stay in the hospital for quite a while. Whenever Josephine went to visit her she had some new escape plan.

'This time Josie, I'm going to wait until it's really windy and then ask if I can go outside in the grounds with my kite. I'm light enough. I know I am. I haven't eaten for days.'

Josephine shook her head slowly and on the way home on

the underground she found herself in tears.

Still, Josephine carried on working and going to the pub and doing the washing-up. On Wednesdays she had dinner with Arthur and on Sundays she visited Fin. When she had a bit of extra money she would buy herself a new dress. Josephine had a closet that was full of clothes she never wore: black tulle, burgundy organza, dresses with hoops, lace. Brightly coloured long kaftans, shiny blue taffeta, a pink satin mini-skirt: Josephine's closet was like a secret garden that an invisible gardener cultivated and no one ever sat in. She would stare down at it from her window, or rather open her closet doors and look at the colours without ever stepping into them.

Josephine had a whole list of shops she frequented during her lunch hour. She found nothing quite so satisfying as spotting a dress that she wanted. After circling around it for days she would finally gather up her courage and take it off the rack. In the fitting room she would stare at herself in the mirror feeling transformed. This was the only time she actually wore these clothes. A paisley frock with a bow at the back, a black cotton shift with slits up the legs, a crêpe-de-chine skirt with a contrasting top: Josephine spent a lot of money on clothes.

One Wednesday when Arthur was over for tea Josephine said to him, 'Arthur, you've been working so hard since Fin went into the hospital. Why don't you go away for a holiday somewhere? Take a break.'

'Me, take a holiday?' replied Arthur. 'But you need a

holiday just as much as I do. Besides, I can't afford one.'

'Oh, that's nonsense. Flights are so cheap these days. You should go away to Spain or somewhere like that. Lie on a beach and go to nightclubs.'

'Josephine, you know I don't like the sun and I hate dancing. Besides, I'd worry about you and Fin. Who'd be here to make sure you're all right? Who'd visit Fin on Tuesdays?'

'But, Arthur,' said Josephine, 'you're too young to be so serious.'

'You should talk, Josefiend, you should talk. You're younger than both Fin and I. It's you who goes about with a long face. Fin and I are perfectly happy. I think you should go away on holiday.'

On Sunday, when Josephine was at the hospital, Fin said, 'Josephine, you look terrible. Take a holiday. Go away and get some sunshine. You worry too much. I'm fine,' she said, giggling. 'I tricked a nurse the other day. For three days I didn't speak. Not one word. Then just when she was getting really fed up with me I asked her which was the way to the nearest exit out of this place. I think she wanted to kill me. Anyway, Josie, you should take a holiday. I'm tired of seeing your worried face every Sunday. Give me a break.' Fin winked.

So Josephine and Arthur decided to go away together. They bought European train tickets and packed their bags. Before they left Fin told them where she had hidden her money when she ran away, so they took that with them as well. On the day of their departure they met at Victoria Station.

'My God Josefiend,' swore Arthur, 'your suitcase is enormous! What have you got in it?'

'Just a few things,' said Josephine quietly.

In Paris, on the Champs-Elysées, Josephine wore scarlet mousseline with a matching bow in her hair; in Lyons, crimson moire with a black beret. On a gondola in Venice she wore an olive gabardine dress that was double-breasted at the front and fitted at the back. Every morning, over the brioche and coffee, Arthur said, 'Wow.' Josephine had never been happier.

They travelled across Europe like two migrating birds, coming to rest wherever they pleased. In Vienna Josephine had to buy a second suitcase which Arthur did not mind having to carry; it made him happy to see his sister relaxed. They sat silently, staring out of the windows of the fast European trains, Josephine's hands folded neatly in her gloves. They travelled beside rivers and along coastlines. Josephine's wardrobe expanded.

After three weeks they returned home to their jobs. That Sunday they went to see Fin together.

'But, you've come back!' cried Fin when she saw them. 'You were meant to escape, not return,' she said, her voice full of anguish as she began to sob. 'Why? Why? Did they catch you? You weren't meant to come back. I thought you'd gone for me.'

Arthur and Josephine stood at the foot of Fin's bed. They

were speechless. Josephine went up to Fin and attempted to put an arm around her heaving shoulders.

'Don't touch me!' Fin shouted. 'You could have gone! Now they'll get you too. If you can escape, why don't you?'

'But Fin,' stuttered Josephine. 'Fin. We had to come back. We've got responsibilities. We've got you.'

'No you haven't!' shouted Fin. 'They've got me. You've got no responsibilities except for those you've made up! You're mad not to escape. Mad!' Arthur took Josephine by the hand.

'We'd better go home Josephine,' he said.

'Yes, you'd better,' shouted Fin.

On the underground Arthur sat with his arm around Josephine. 'Maybe she's right,' he said.

'Right about what?' snapped Josephine. 'We can't stay on holiday forever.'

'No, but maybe we should leave.'

'Why?'

'I don't know. Maybe Fin knows something we don't.'

'I'm sure she does Arthur. She must do.' When they reached the next stop they said goodbye and Josephine got off the train. She walked up the street to her flat very slowly. Sunday afternoon was dead in London; everyone had bought their newspapers and shut the door. Josephine made herself a cup of tea then went into her bedroom. She opened her closet doors and stood looking at the colour of her clothes. Then she climbed into the wardrobe and closed the doors behind her.

The Battersea Power Station

S he said out loud to the man conducting the job
interview,

'I had to give up my black leather jacket when I realised it
had once been animate. I gave it back to its rightful owner,
some cow I never met.' And then she said,

'Yeah. We met on the underground. We spent the night
snorting cocaine and fucking in the Battersea Power
Station.' She continued with, 'No, I don't eat much any
more. I kept wondering if it's really fair to eat vegetables.
Maybe they have a right to live too. Right now I'm trying
hard to work out some way for me to live by photosynthesis. But the sun never seems to shine any more.' Then she
smiled and told him her best joke.

'What do you call a man standing in a pot of ratatouille?
Basil.' She laughed away to herself. Then, she collected her
things and said she had to go home and scare the rats out of
the kitchen. She put on her jacket, tearing the lining again,
and walked off. She walked through Covent Garden
oblivious. She hated it there so she pretended she wasn't
there at all. She smiled at the bags of shopping as if they
were people and looked at the people as if they were bags of

shopping, which some of them actually were. On the Strand she got on a bus. A man sat next to her; it was the man she had met on the underground. He said,

'I quit my job today. My boss underpays me, he fiddles the books, gives people dead turkeys at Christmas, and expects them to be happy. Dead turkeys. I can't believe it. Most people need money.'

'Jobs don't matter anyway,' she said. 'It's a bad thing, doing what you're told to do. You can go on the dole and eat chocolate.'

They got off the bus at the Battersea Power Station and snorted cocaine and fucked all night. When dawn crept through the grimy windows of the control room, he said to her,

'We mustn't snort this stuff, you know. It probably comes from South America or Asia or somewhere and they probably force people to grow it when they should be growing vegetables to eat.'

'Vegetables,' she said. 'Dead turkeys, vegetables, my black leather jacket.'

'You'd look good in a black leather jacket,' he said.

'What do you call a man with a car on his head? Jack.' She said this and sighed and touched the boy from the underground with the back of her hand. 'Maybe photosynthesis is a bad idea, maybe I can survive on sex alone.' So, in the name of scientific experiment, they started to fuck again, while in the boiler room some slime grew, the pigeons cooed, and the girders rusted.

The next day was sunny, so she stretched out on the roof garden and smiled at the sun. With her legs spread-eagled, her arms fully extended, her fingers and toes spread and stretching, her eyes closed, and her gums exposed, she tried very hard to photosynthesise. Just in case she could not live by fucking alone. The sun felt great, all over her body.

After a while one of her flatmates came up on to the garden and said, 'Hey. What are you doing?' She just smiled, exposing her gums a little more. The flatmate said, 'Do you want something to eat?' She shook her head. The flatmate went away. Soon she could smell cooking. She wondered what her flatmate had killed. She got up off the roof, looking hopefully at her arm for a tinge of green, then went down to her room. She fumbled around in the closet for a dress and pulled out a suede jacket instead. Oh no. She sighed to herself, then took it into the sitting-room where her flatmates were devouring things and said,

'Look at this. I'd forgotten all about it. What am I going to do with it, whose is it, does it come from Jersey, Hereford, or Loseley? Some cow I never met.' She smiled at her flatmates and did a brief tap dance. 'What do you call a girl with two eggs, chips, beans, toast, and tea on her head? Caf.' Then she danced away before they could catch her. She walked to the National Film Theatre and watched a Fred Astaire movie. When the lights came on she discovered she was sitting next to the man from the underground. They got on his push-bike, she sat on the seat, he stood and pedalled, and they rode to the Battersea Power Station. 23

From Nine Elms Lane it looms like eternity. Even at night it casts a gothic shadow. He called to her as they rode along, turning his head so the wind would catch his words and carry them to her.

'Being unemployed is like waiting for a train. The train never comes so you amuse yourself by reading the posters backwards. You get to know the posters very well. Soon these posters start to excite you. You are sure they are trying to tell you something, not just about the product, but something about the meaning of life. I'm glad I'm unemployed. It gives me a greater understanding of things.'

'Being unemployed makes me worry about eating,' she said.

Then they were inside the Battersea Power Station, up in the control room, fucking on the parquet floor, reading the dials on the walls when they paused. He said,

'Why do we fuck on the parquet floor?'

'Because the boiler room is too scary,' she replied. Then she giggled and said, 'Oh, my suede jacket,' as if those words had meaning, and he said,

'You'd look good in a suede jacket.' Later, when they leaned against the cut-glass windows overlooking the boiler room she said,

'What do you call a man with a pigeon on his head? Cliff. Or Nelson.'

The next day was rainy so she sat in the kitchen and cut up the newspaper and put it back together but with the sentences, paragraphs, articles all mixed up so there was an article on how to holiday in Israel on the overseas news page and an article about the ANC on the entertainment page. One of her flatmates came in and offered to cook her breakfast but she said,

'No, thank you. I am trying to survive on sex alone. Not just ordinary sex, of course, but sex with the man from the underground in the Battersea Power Station. You must understand the connection there. Sex – energy – power – fuel – electricity – you know, all those things. Sex in the Battersea Power Station, that should be enough, don't you think?' Then she put on her favourite dress and walked to the British Museum. Peering into a mummy case she saw the face of the boy from the underground. She turned around and he was there. He took her in his arms and they did a slow waltz through the room full of large, wonderful, Egyptian things, past the art deco porcelain and into the room with the sixteenth-century religious icons. They zigzagged through history like a sewing machine and came to rest in front of Oscar Wilde's handwritten manuscript of *The Importance of Being Earnest* and she cried to the museum guard who stood watching.

'We will go down in histrionics,' then she laughed and they salsaed all the way to the Battersea Power Station and fucked on the floor of the boiler room. They looked up at the decaying girders and columns, they listened to the pigeons cooing, and the water that ran along the floor collected in a pool around them. His voice echoed through the enormous chamber when he said,

'Being with you is like being with a spirit. Being with you is like just catching a train. Being with you is like riding downhill,' and she said,

'Thanks, I like you too. You always show up at the right time.' They kissed for a while and the Battersea Power Station groaned from disuse. Then she said,

'What do you call a man with a bog on his head? Pete.' They laughed and then after a while he said,

'That's my name.'

Lois and The Ancients

Lois's life has been punctuated by Egyptian hieroglyphics. Its various stages have been marked by strange
involvements with cryptic designs from the ancient people
of the Nile. For Lois, the writing on the wall is literally that
of the blue Egyptian beetle, straight out of the Book of the
Dead.

There is a photograph of Lois that was taken during her
trip to Egypt. She is standing inside a tomb in the Valley of
the Kings. The photograph is very dark but the symbols on
the wall directly behind her are still visible. The columns of
pictographs end halfway up Lois's legs and then, stretching
across the wall, a banquet is depicted, complete with naked
serving girls ministering to those dark, androgynous beau-
ties who seem to have made up the Egyptian ruling classes.
On Lois's right in the photograph stands the boyfriend she
was travelling with at the time. He has struck what he
considered to be a typical ancient Egyptian pose: his arms
and legs are all bent at opposing angles, jutting out in a sort
of bony and humorous version of a swastika.

In this photograph Lois herself is peering at the camera.
She looks small, young, and like a tourist. She is sunburnt,

round and very unlike the ancients who pose in straight lines over her head, or the modern Egyptians who wait patiently outside the tomb for her to pay them. Lois's affinity is with the symbols on the walls but it is not obvious in this or other photographs.

Lois has no Egyptian connections, as far as she knows. She is the granddaughter of farmworkers and history has never been one of her interests. She has no obvious link to the Book of the Dead. Ordinarily, Lois lives her life like most people and she is only very occasionally prone to acts of deviance. On a quiet Wednesday morning in the British Museum she once climbed into an Egyptian sarcophagus. She lay on her back on the cold timeless stone for a few brief moments before climbing back out.

The most serious problem in Lois's relatively problem-free life is that she has terrible trouble trying to find somewhere to live. The rental market dealing in small self-contained flats is out of her reach financially and the local housing bodies all see her as too single, too able, too young, and too uninsistent to house. So Lois has had to be content with the shifting, precarious, and increasingly less legal existence of a squatter. Her clothes, her bed, and her box of photographs and postcards from her one trip out of the country have moved with her from derelict property to boarded-up flat to unserviced nightmare and back again.

This unsettling lifestyle does not suit Lois at all. She is the kind of person who likes to know where she will be in three
months' time, a not unusual personality trait, even amongst

the young. Lois feels every time she gets her room sorted out, the photos and postcards stuck on the wall and her bed comfortably arranged, she has to pack it all up again and move on. This makes Lois nervous and unhappy.

'Let's move into this house,' Lois said to her friend Clara as they wandered around gazing into other people's warm sitting-rooms.

'Why this house?' asks Clara. She, too, is tired of moving.

'It looks nice. We could get in through the back. It probably has electricity and everything.'

'Who do you think owns it? We want to be careful this time. No more moving into empty houses that belong to that Duke, or Lord, or whatever he is. He'll have us out in an instant, just like before.'

'That's right. I don't think he owns anything around here though,' Lois said to Clara, staring up at the house's big windows, her eyes following the unbroken line of the guttering. She was trying to imagine what the house was like inside and what she would look like in it, what it would be like to live there. 'It's kind of posh around here, Clara. The pavements are so clean.'

'Mmm. The neighbours won't be used to squatters. They'll probably form a vigilante group and hound us out in the middle of the night, like the time before last.'

'No,' said Lois, 'that was the time before the time before.'

'Oh,' said Clara, 'well, that's probably what they'll do anyway.'

While Lois and Clara stood outside the house and talked 29

they watched what went on in the quiet street. Eventually they decided to move into the house.

They got in through the back late that night, and then changed the lock of the front door. That took all night and so it was the next morning when Lois brought all her belongings to the house with the help of a friend with a van. Clara had put a piece of paper on the front door. It said, 'This property is legally occupied'.

Lois said to Clara, 'That sign will bring us to the attention of the neighbours. Let's take it down and hope they don't notice us. We only want to lead quiet lives, after all.'

'All right,' said Clara, and she went outside and took the sign down.

The house was very big and lovely with large, airy rooms and high ceilings. The services were all on and functioning and there were even carpets in one or two of the rooms. Everything about the house was in remarkably good shape, especially considering its age and that it had been empty for several years. Lois and Clara settled down to a springtime of home improvements. They did a bit of work on the garden and tried to dry out the basement which suffered from damp rising from no one knew where.

Without knowing who owned the house or what its fate, together with theirs, might be they worked on becoming more and more at home. Lois felt particularly attached to her bedroom. As the summer warmed up, her room remained cool, and there was always a sepulchral silence in it. The walls were panelled with dark heavy wood and were tremendously thick. Sunlight never fell on the north-facing rooms of the house, but they were well lit artificially. Lois felt happy there. She arranged her postcards of mummies and sphinxes on the wall in a way that pleased her and, as the summer progressed and she spent more time in the garden, she began to take on that round and sunburnt look that she had had in the photograph, which she stuck on to her wall as well.

Late one night, Lois awoke suddenly. She sat up, turned her light on and looked around the room. Getting out of bed and putting on her clothes, she walked to the furthest wall in the room, the one adjacent to the windows where the fireplace must have been. Lois decided that it was time for the heavy wooden panelling to come off the walls. She went downstairs to find the hammer, crow-bar, and wedge, then she set about carefully prizing the panelling off the wall.

The panelling itself was very old; it had probably been on the walls for several hundred years. The nails were thick and square and the plaster of the wall beneath was solid. Lois strained and banged and pulled for a long time before the first panel gave slightly. Just as it was beginning to come away, Clara walked into the room.

'What are you doing Lois?' she asked, rubbing her eyes and yawning. 'It's terribly late. I thought we were still working on the basement. It seems a shame to start something new before we've finished down there.'

'I want to get rid of these panels. They're too dark,' Lois said, although she wasn't really sure why she was taking 31 them down.

'Oh,' said Clara, 'I like those panels. We could have traded rooms; mine doesn't have any panelling.'

'No, I like this room, I want to stay in it. I don't like these panels though. You can have them after I take them down.' Lois was attempting to be very methodical and careful about removing the panels but, even so, as one came away there were splinters and sawdust.

'All right then,' Clara said walking out of the room. 'I'm going back to bed.'

A few minutes after Clara was gone, Lois succeeded in pulling the first panel off the wall. An enormous cloud of dust came out from underneath it, filling Lois's eyes and nose and smelling powerfully of the past. Lois kept working despite being unable to see properly and the panelling started to come away much more quickly once the first bit was removed. Every time she pulled a piece of the heavy wood away from the wall another large cloud of dust would come whooshing out. Lois got dirtier and dirtier and her eyes became reddened and sore. The smell grew stronger. It was a dry, musty smell that spoke of years of preservation, reminding Lois of something very particular that she could not quite place.

As soon as she got the last panel down Lois went off to have a bath, before the dust had settled. She shook herself out in the garden before getting into the warm water, then scrubbed her skin and shampooed her hair. Her body felt coated in dust and, despite her soaps and flannels, it continued to cling to her. Lois felt it was inside her body as well, filling her lungs and abdominal cavity. She drew the bath a second time and went through the whole process again. Once she had finished she felt marginally cleaner so she got out of the bath and dried herself off. She filled the tub again and dumped her clothes into it, then, clad in her towel, climbed the stairs back up to her bedroom. By then it was after dawn. Lois's entire room was covered in the thick disentombed dust: her bed, her clothes, the carpet. The smell was thick as well.

The panels were stacked in a pile where Lois had laid them, one by one, as she prised them away. The wall itself was there for Lois to gaze upon now. There were the vertical lines of hieroglyphics, scarab, bird, eye, lotus; there were the tall and slender men and women with that impenetrable, passive, and, at the same time, commanding expression on their faces; their sandalled feet, their bejewelled ears and necks, their exquisitely long and lean arms stretching out towards the offerings of the naked serving girls or themselves making offerings to the mummies who were encased in gold and surrounded by jackal headed minions.

Lois stood and looked at the wall for a long time, finally remembering where she had smelled the dust before. It was the same smell that hung in the air of the tombs in the Valley of the Kings. Ancient, dry, and scented ever so faintly with fragrant oils, paint, and gold: the smell of mummies and the wealthy dead. Lois went over to her bed and shook out the bedclothes. She climbed in underneath them and closed her eyes. In her last thoughts before she fell asleep she wondered who owned the house in which she was living and how long it would be before she and Clara were evicted.

The Unbearable Shortness
of Holidays

In Perugia all sensibility is lost. It floats away on the warm sectarian breeze that drifts up from the South becoming thinner and thinner as it crosses Europe. For the out-of-town, out-of-country visitor this hill-top town, surrounded by rich and fragrant farmland, can seem like nirvana.

'Ah,' sighed the tourist, 'there is no hurly-burly here.'

'Mmm,' sighed the other tourist, 'the only hustle is the evening rounds of the cafés and even then one can always find a seat.'

'Mmm.' The two tourists were in reflective mode, which they termed as the Italian mode. 'Somewhere someone must be working,' said one tourist to the other as she opened her lazy eyes and took a languid look around. 'But I can't see who.'

'Well,' the other replied, 'it's not me.' They both sighed again and went back to sleep over their Cinzano in the mid-day sun.

In Perugia the tourist need not be intrepid to discover the joys of the local environs. The cafés, bars and restaurants are easy to find; the atmosphere lulls without any effort. The wine is in the shops, the smell of flowers in the air, the doors of the churches open, and the lanes and byways are to be walked through. There is even a Roman aqueduct, conveniently placed across the fuchsia-laden slope. You don't have to look for anything – an indolent tourist's dream come true.

The day began like this: six o'clock, it was sunny, Elena woke up. The pigeons were cooing loudly, a cool breeze came through the shutters on the window. 'My God,' Elena thought, 'another day here. Another day away from my job. Another day to drink Campari and wear dark glasses and smile. My God.' She lay still in her narrow bed listening to the morning sounds that drifted through her window.

In the next bed Lucia lay sleeping. The two women had adopted Italian names for the duration of the holiday. In fact, Lucia was dreaming that she was an Italian running through a field of mimosa. At one end of the field a small village fair was taking place. There was only one table at the fair. It was draped with a banner that read, 'The Revolutionary Communist Party of Italy'. The table was laden with food. The Italian communists were selling Gnocchi alla Gorgonzola – little balls of heaven smothered in blue, briny delight. Lucia smiled in her sleep.

After another hour the two women had risen and were making their way through the morning rituals of showering and dressing. Elena kept collapsing on to the bed with her copy of *L'Uomo*, a men's fashion magazine. Lucia was trying to read Shelley but found she could not concentrate whatever the time of day, the lazy morning, the quiet afternoon, nor the peaceful evening. Every day in the café she would bring out her book and begin to read. 'Many a green isle needs must be/In the deep wide sea of Misery', and every day she yawned and stretched and looked up from her book at the people passing by.

'Elena,' she said, 'I can't concentrate on anything, not even a poem.'

'No,' said Elena, who didn't attempt to read, 'there's too much to look at, smell and drink.'

After dressing, the two women floated out of their pensione and wandered over to the coffee bar where they ate custard-filled pastries and drank cappuccino, weak tea and juice for breakfast. They stood inside the coffee bar while they ate, alongside the older men, cloth-capped and short, and the younger women who were smartly dressed for business. The tourists' eyes were steamed open by the coffee machine which hissed and puffed as they stood without speaking, listening to the morning conversation around them. What did the words these Italians used mean as they flew back and forth over the sleepy heads of Elena and Lucia? The elderly man in the felt vest – was he talking about the weather which was perfect, or the coffee which was aromatic, or the day ahead which to Elena and Lucia seemed magical? Or was he talking about politics and the strength of the Italian economy, 'Il Sorpasso', the money in the North and the poverty in the South? And what did he do during the war?

Elena was nodding off over her coffee so Lucia suggested 37

they get another cup from the busy man behind the coffee bar and move to one of the rickety tables outside. There they sat in the morning sun, Elena napping behind her dark glasses, Lucia examining an English newspaper.

'Home has never looked so bleak,' Lucia said to Elena. 'I can't imagine why I live there.' Elena, looking up, let her dark glasses slide to the tip of her nose so she could peer over them at Lucia.

'You live there, Lucia, because it is home,' she replied, pushing her dark glasses back up on to the bridge of her nose.

'Yes, of course, it is home. But it does seem terrible from here. Look at this weather report. It has been raining all week and will continue to rain all next week. The government is introducing austerity to the poor – isn't that a bit like introducing the Pope to God? Look at this Elena, look at this,' Lucia said, holding up the newspaper and pointing at the headline, MASS SUICIDE ON LONDON BRIDGE: TWENTY BROKERS DEAD. Can you explain that?'

'They'd probably been caught fiddling or something,' Elena replied. 'I wonder how high the suicide rate is here?'

'Suicide?' she laughed. 'In heaven?' She shook her head.

'Lucia,' Elena said firmly, lowering her dark glasses once more. 'One tourist's heaven can be a resident's hell.'

'Hmm,' muttered Lucia folding up her newspaper and resolving not to buy another. After sipping her coffee she cleared her throat and, simultaneously, cleared her mind of unemployment, racism, and decline.

Elena and Lucia spent their days repeating a seemingly endless cycle of enormously pleasurable activities. They would rise, breakfast, and then spend the morning wandering around Perugia with their mouths open. They looked in the shops, toured the churches, wandered along the hillside spotting remnants of the Etruscan city from a time before. They sniffed the scented breeze and followed their noses to a shop where they bought food for a picnic lunch: olives, artichokes, marinated tomatoes, bread, Gorgonzola and Orvieto vino bianco secco. Then they'd find a park or a piece of grass in a churchyard where they would sit in the sun and eat and drink and maybe chat to other tourists while quietly and slowly falling asleep. The mid-day zephyr would play along the hem of Elena's skirt, sliding up her leg like a warm hand. Lucia dreamed of Mario Lanza; she could hear 'Ave Maria' in her sleep.

After a while they gathered their things and walked back up to the town centre, climbing the narrow steps that wind up through the buildings, past medieval churches and under Etruscan arches. Perugia is like that, all up and down, steps instead of streets; there is a lift that travels from one part of town up on the hill to another part down below. The tourist stumbles upon sudden views; rounding a corner you are greeted by the valley and surrounding hills. They call out to you like a dream of Italy, too lovely to be real. The poplars stand straight like boy soldiers; the tourist can lead an enchanted life, not like home at all.

Back in the huge cobbled square that forms the town

centre Lucia and Elena would spend the rest of the afternoon sitting in one of the six or seven outdoor cafés that line the square. They'd nibble on bar snacks and drink Cinzano and Campari and aqua minerale and coffee whilst attempting to read or write on postcards. They'd speak in broken English to the people at the next table, foreigners studying at the University for Strangers, one of the city's institutes of learning. Elena felt that she wanted to move to Perugia and be a stranger at the university herself.

The afternoon sun shone down on the town square. Lucia hiked her dress up, exposing her brown legs. 'Elena,' she said, 'I don't want to go home.'

'Neither do I, neither do I.'

'Maybe we could ring up our bosses and tell them we're not coming back. We could ring our banks and have them transfer our accounts to the Bank of Perugia. We could find someone to move into our flats. Then we could stay here forever. Growing old in Perugia, Elena, we won't get rheumatism here! We won't end up starving on tiny pensions. Oh, oh, we can be Italians and wear dark glasses and study Gramsci and discuss Fellini and eat fettucini Alfredo until we die!'

Elena opened her eyes. 'Lucia,' she said, 'this is a holiday. We are tourists. Life isn't like this, Italy isn't like this. How would we live, we'd have to get jobs, who'd be our friends, what about our responsibilities?' Elena sighed and shook her head slowly in the afternoon sun. 'We're tourists here.'

Lucia sighed then as well, feeling great sadness as she stared into her Martini bianco. Life seemed so perfect.

The afternoon became early evening and the two women left the café and walked back to the pensione. Once again, they showered and dressed with the windows wide open on to the sunset. The smell of cooking floated up from a kitchen nearby as they headed off to find a restaurant for dinner. Lucia and Elena would spend a good hour examining menus and debating about where they should eat.

'Bruschetta,' said Elena. 'I demand bruschetta. It's bruschetta or nothing, I swear!'

'Mmm,' said Lucia, 'I want zucchini. I want tortellini. I want it all!' Eventually, they settled on somewhere and had a long and drawn-out meal, arguing with the people at the next table while being either charmed or ignored by the waiters. Around midnight they made their way home, giggling as they tripped on the cobblestones, stopping for gelati on the way. The next day they woke up early and everything began again.

Eventually, the day came when the return flight was scheduled to take off and no matter how much they objected, swearing to the skies and cursing the great God of Work, they were on it, like dutiful daughters.

The next year Elena and Lucia met in a London pub to plan their forthcoming holiday. It was a dark and raining February night.

'Well, where shall we go this year my dear?' Elena asked Lucia.

'To Italy, of course!' replied Lucia, shocked by Elena's

question which she felt implied there was an alternative. 'We'll go to Perugia.'

'Again?' said Elena.

'What do you mean, "again"?' said Lucia, her voice full of surprise and hurt.

'Well, we could go to Greece and sun ourselves amongst the ruins, or we could go to Spain and eat paella, or even Portugal, I hear it's nice and not crowded.'

'But what about the cafés in the town square? What about our walks on the hills? Our day trips to Lago Trasimere?' Lucia stared into her pint of beer moodily. Two months later she and Elena were on the plane, heading for Perugia.

When they arrived they found the very same little pensione where they'd stayed the previous year. The first evening they went back to their favourite restaurant where the head waiter recognised them, greeting them by name. Lucia smiled broadly at Elena once they were seated.

'Ah, it is paradise. Aren't you pleased that I was so keen to come back? We'll have a wonderful fortnight, I know it.'

'Yes,' replied Elena. 'We will.' They spent the evening lingering over a tremendous meal and then stopped for gelati as they stumbled home.

In the morning, they awoke early as the birds began to sing and the first rays of sun broke through. The sounds of the town filtered up into their room. Lucia stretched her limbs out on the bed. Elena was already up, getting ready for a shower.

'I think,' said Lucia, 'I think I'll have a gelato for breakfast.'

'A what?' replied Elena, aghast.

'A gelato, Elena. I want a gelato for breakfast. A pink one. Then we can go and have the brioche and coffee like we always do.'

'A gelato,' said Elena thoughtfully. 'Well, why not? You're on holiday, you can have whatever you want!'

So the two women set off to find Lucia ice-cream for breakfast. Luckily, one eager entrepreneur had anticipated this foreigner's early morning urge for sweetness and had opened his gelato counter at dawn. Lucia asked him for a pink one, a triple, and they sat on the steps of the medieval town hall while she ate it. The sun grew steadily stronger while the two women made their way to a coffee bar where they stood in the steam of the espresso machine and drank cups of hot coffee and ate brioche. They spent the morning reacquainting themselves with Perugia and then, as before, bought themselves the ingredients of a picnic for lunch. Taking a bus out of town, they disembarked at the first poppy-covered hill they saw and, sitting in the shade of a Lombardy poplar, ate.

'The air is so soft,' Lucia said, 'it's like ice-cream. Soft and smooth and delicious.'

'Ice-cream?' said Elena, slightly annoyed. 'But ice-cream is cold and here the air is so warm.'

'Like warm ice-cream then,' replied Lucia, her head tilted back and her face in the sun. 'Melted.'

They spent the afternoon dozing on the hillside, listening to the sounds of the country. In the distance a farmer was toiling. He glanced their way from time to time.

At about half-past four they arose and began to walk back into Perugia. Three-quarters of the way there Lucia said, 'When we get back into town, do you know what I'd like?'

'A Cinzano,' said Elena greedily. 'Or maybe a Campari. Vino bianco. Vino rosso . . . vino . . .'

'A gelato,' interrupted Lucia. 'A green one.' Then she smiled to herself, a large benevolent grin, the fat smile of a happy woman.

'And you shall have it, I decree,' replied Elena. When they reached the town they wandered towards the centre through the cobblestone byways and up the narrow staircases. Then they found a table at a café in the town square. When the waiter came over to them, Elena asked for a Martini bianco secco and Lucia asked for gelato, the green kind, in a dish with whipped cream. They sat in the late-afternoon sun and laughed at each other.

The next morning after they'd showered and dressed and were on their way to breakfast, Lucia made a slight detour into the corner shop where she persuaded the proprietor, with broken Italian and much gesticulating, to sell her a gelato. Elena had assumed that Lucia had gone into the shop for something much more basic, like tampons or tissues, but tried not to show her surprise. Lucia ate the ice-cream like a starved person as they walked in the direction of the coffee bars.

The same thing happened on the way to their lunch-time picnic and then, as they were making a tour of the restaurant menus trying to decide where to have their evening meal, Lucia slipped away while Elena was musing over the tortellini and came back licking a gelato. A blue one this time.

'Lucia!' exclaimed Elena, alarmed. 'Another gelato?'

'So?' she replied defensively. 'Another gelato, so what? I like them. Do you mind?'

'Not at all, my dear, but it would spoil my appetite.'

'Well, it doesn't spoil mine,' answered Lucia. 'Not one bit.'

Over the course of the next couple of days Lucia ate more Italian ice-cream than most Italians would eat in a month, maybe even a year. She ate all the flavours of gelati she could find then she began to comb the city for more. Pistachio, lemon, orange, fruit, coffee, rum, chocolate, amaretto, strawberry, peach, chocolate-chip, blueberry, blackberry, and all the alcoholic varieties: Lucia was compiling a mental list. On the occasions she was unable to find a new flavour she was not put off, but would take the opportunity to reassess what she'd thought of it the first time.

Elena watched with increasing dismay. She tried to curb her friend's new habit with subtlety at first.

'Too much sugar is not good for your skin,' she said gently.

To which Lucia replied, 'So what?'

'Too many dairy products are not good for your blood or your digestion.'

To which Lucia replied, 'Bollocks.'

'You'll get ice-cream gag,' she tried one afternoon mid-gelato, 'and then you'll never want to eat it again.'

'No way,' replied Lucia. 'That will never happen to me. I love it too much.'

'You're telling me,' whispered Elena under her breath.

In the early evening of the fourth day when Lucia was about to embark on her sixth gelato of the day, Elena could stand it no longer. 'YOU'LL GET FAT!' she shouted as loudly as she could.

'I DON'T CARE!' shouted Lucia back.

The next morning Elena packed up her belongings and moved to another room in the pensione. She began to tour Perugia and the environs on her own. She took a day-trip to Florence and stood and stared at Michelangelo's David for several hours. She travelled around the countryside swimming in the gentle lakes and walking over the quiet hills. One day she went to Assisi to see the frescoes of Giotto. There she met an Englishman who offered to buy her a gelato. She thanked him but said no and took the bus back to Perugia. Then she went looking for her friend.

Lucia was seated at a café in the square. She'd grown quite brown in the days since Elena had seen her last. In front of her on the table was a large silver bowl full of ice-cream, fruit and whipped cream. When Elena spotted her she was poised to dive into it with a big silver spoon.

'Hello there,' said Elena. 'How are you?'

Lucia dropped her spoon. It fell into the whipped cream and disappeared like a plane flying into a cloud. She looked up at Elena and then back down at the ice-cream. 'Hello,' she said without looking back up. 'Where did it go?'

'Look,' said Elena assertively. 'I've got something to say to you.'

'Oh don't bother. I know what it is already. Well, I'm not going home this time. I'm not going back to that dark mucky place. The ice-cream is lousy there.'

'I'm not asking you to come back,' said Elena. 'What I'm asking is why. Why are you doing it this way? You could have found a quicker way.'

'A quicker way to what?' asked Lucia, looking up. 'A quicker way to eat ice-cream?'

'No, a quicker way to freeze time,' she replied.

Lucia looked back down at her ice-cream. The swirls of colour, cheerful bits of fruit, and mountains of whipped cream looked heavenly to her. In the ice-cream she could see a better world, one that would fit her, that she could eat up and feel happy in. In gelato there is certainty, a priceless commodity in a post-modern world. 'I don't want it to melt away,' she said to Elena who remained impassive behind her dark glasses.

'Neither do I, Lucia, neither do I.'

The Fact-Finding Mission

Dora came home and found the note on the kitchen table. It said, in large bold letters, THE ENGLISH ARE REPRESSED BECAUSE THEY HAVE NO LAKES. Dora sighed when she read this and wondered if it was true. There are a few lakes, somewhere, but they are all kept in the Lake District, as if one can't allow lakes just anywhere. If lakes are not kept where they belong everyone might start throwing off their clothes and jumping in and we all know where that would lead.

Dora sighed and sat down. She was very tired. She had been out on one of her fact-finding missions. As usual, she had found there were no facts to find. 'One day,' thought Dora, 'one day I'll give up my search and then where will we all be?' She sighed again, then picked up the note and turned it over. On the other side it said, THE ENGLISH ARE REPRESSED BECAUSE THEY HAVE NO MOUNTAINS. 'No mountains and no lakes,' thought Dora. 'How true.' She slumped off to bed.

In the morning Dora got up, not at all refreshed, and set off on one of her fact-finding missions again. Dora strove to find facts nearly every day now. She felt she was being driven mad by misinformation. 'There are so many lies everywhere,' she often said. 'They are lying about everything these days. Wars, identities, deaths. I can't believe anything. I must seek out the facts. I must find out the truth.'

Dora knew she was being a bit ridiculous, but she was unemployed so that kind of thing didn't matter to her. Besides, when she set out on her fact-finding missions she felt really terrific, like Simone de Beauvoir, or Mrs Emma Peel, or Isabella Bird. She'd put on her favourite clothes and pretend the No. 77 bus was a Bat-bus and that her umbrella had a gun in it. Not that Dora would ever actually try to shoot anyone. Well, no one, except of course, the Liars, if she could find them, wherever and whoever they are.

Dora took the No. 77 bus up the Strand and got out in front of the High Court. She already knew there were no truths, or facts, there but she went anyway, from time to time, just in case. As she was about to head through the doors, she spotted a note on the wall. It said, YOU HATE THE NEW TELECOM PHONE KIOSKS MERELY BECAUSE YOU ARE RESISTANT TO CHANGE. On reading this Dora knew she would not find any facts that day, so she gave up before she had started and walked down the Strand towards Waterloo Bridge, where there are no facts, only sandwich bars and shops selling briefcases.

Dora had been unemployed for rather a long time. She was very poor and her activities were restricted for the most part to listening to the radio, fact-finding missions, talking to friends and other free or very cheap things, like walking in the rain, making up theories about her compatriots, and worrying. She did a lot of the latter. Her friends in work found her increasingly difficult. No one could understand these fact-finding missions.

'Except the person or persons who keep leaving me those notes,' said Dora aloud in the kitchen. She sighed heavily. 'When will I find the place where the facts are? When will I discover where the truth is kept? In the same place as they keep the jobs, I'll bet.' She decided to go and see one of her friends.

Dora went to visit Nora, who lived just around the corner. Nora had also been unemployed for a very long time and she had recently decided to give up applying for jobs and devote her life to the pursuit of complete happiness. This did not involve happiness-finding missions, but it did involve a lot of soul-searching and some heavy-duty reading. Nora was slowly realising that she could not actually afford anything that she thought would give her complete happiness, like a trip to the Soviet Union, for example.

'Oh Nora,' said Dora, 'you're so materialistic. Happiness is one of the free things.'

'Shut up Dora,' screamed Nora, 'it is not! Happiness costs lots and lots of money, and besides, wanting to fly to Rio isn't materialistic. Don't try to tell me that your fact-finding missions make you happy. I have the ease in life, but none of the good things to enjoy in that ease. I have the leisure, but none of the leisurables. I can't even afford to play squash!'

'Oh Nora,' said Dora, 'Don't be so miserable. I didn't know you were so miserable. If only I could tell you the facts. If only I could explain things.'

'Dora,' said Nora, 'you're a real dreamer. Even more of a dreamer than I am. At least I'm trying to pursue something that will get me somewhere.'

'Oh,' said Dora. She felt rather depressed. She got up and kissed Nora on the cheek and then left. As she was unlocking her bicycle, she saw the note taped to the cross-bar. It said, THE ARISTOCRACY IS EXPANDING AT THE SPEED OF LIGHT. Dora got on her bicycle and rode home.

When Dora got home, she took a bath. As she lay there in the hot water, she thought about Nora and what she had said that morning. Dora didn't think Nora was being very realistic.

'How can you find complete happiness if you don't know the facts? How could you ever be sure that what it was that gave you complete happiness wasn't, in fact, something horrible and monstrous? Factually unsubstantiated happiness would be so risky: any day you might find out the facts and bang! your happiness would be gone.' Dora submerged herself in the bath water. She wished she understood things better.

When Dora got out of the bath she found a note pinned to her towel. It said, ALL HISTORY IS THE SAME: RUTHLESS, BITTER, AND MEANINGLESS. 'Ha!' thought Dora, 'is that a fact?' She dried herself off and went into her room and tried to plan the next day's fact-finding missions. But she was running low on ideas and decided to get back into the bath. When she got out of the bath again, quite a while later, there was another note pinned to her towel. It said, THE UNEMPLOYED WRINKLE MORE EASILY THAN THE EMPLOYED.

Dora got up the next day and thought about what she should do. So far that month she'd been to The City, Highgate Cemetery, The Granville Arcade, Southwark Town Hall, The British Library, Hyper-Hyper, the Centrale Café, 'Cats', several branches of W.H. Smith, Kennington Police Station, the Polytechnic of Central London, and many, many other places, each of which had seemed potential and, in some cases, promising fact-sources until Dora actually investigated them. At the end of each mission she was always forced to conclude the same thing: that facts are, indeed, elusive little items.

So, Dora decided she would ride the Circle Line until she found the truth. She got on at Victoria and began to circle central London hoping to pick up some facts rather like a vulture circles its prey. At Paddington she noticed the note stuck on the window behind her. It said, THERE IS NO SUCH THING AS A FACT; ALL THAT EXISTS IS ABSOLUTE FICTION.

Dora read this note and then read it again. She sat on her seat on the Circle Line train and wondered if the note was true. If it was true it meant that she would now have nothing to do every day, no mission in life, no reason to get up. So, Dora chose to ignore it, as people ignore even the most obvious of messages. The Circle Line carried Dora away from Paddington Station. And then, eventually, it brought her back again.

Charlie

Charlie did not like the Royal Family because she did not want to sleep with any of them. Not a one. Not even the little ones. What use was a Royal Family, repository of the nation's fantasies, when you couldn't fancy them? No use at all. Charlie was a republican.

Charlie's mother had named her Charlotte, after Prince Charles. It was better than Andrea, or Edwina, she supposed. Her mother thought Anne too plain. Princess Anne, the one who looks like a horse. The one who is a horse. The only one with any self-respect. A maelstrom of divorce had hit that family. Too bloody rich.

Most of the time, Charlie did not think about that family at all. Sometimes she ran into them, at film previews in Leicester Square, inaugurating hospitals and clinics. They were there, doing their stuff, and Charlie happened by. They'd wave at her in the crowd, and she'd shrug her shoulders. She didn't want any of their waves.

She had to admit it though, she had had sex with Prince Charles a couple of times. It made her bad-tempered just to think of it. It was after his wife Diana had discovered he was
still in love with Camilla Parker-Bowles, his old girlfriend.

Diana had thrown a frying pan at him, and he'd agreed to stop seeing Camilla. It came out later that he'd had his fingers crossed behind his back, but decided to give Parker-Bowles a wide margin for a while anyway. During these boring, non-love-sexy times, Charles tended to frequent Irish pubs in Camden, a part of north London that smells of beer and rotting vegetables. He travelled incognito, disguised as an Irishman.

Charlie herself went to Irish pubs for the crack, for the music. That night the bar was so crowded she could hardly move. Everyone kept burning each other's hair with their fags. Charlie drank whiskey, and Prince Charles trod on her foot. At the time she didn't know who he was, but she left with him anyway.

He kept on his disguise – a black wig, sideburns, little round dark glasses, and a cool leather hat – and shagged her up against a tree. She made him use a condom, she was paranoid about condoms and carried loads around all the time, and he wasn't too pleased. His fake accent slipped as he came, and that was when she realised who he was. She did not have an orgasm, never having liked the royal family. And she told him so.

'I've never liked you lot, you know.'

'Sorry?'

'My mum named me after you, but that doesn't mean I've sworn my allegiance or any such thing.'

Prince Charles mumbled something then, Charlie wasn't sure what. She could tell he didn't do this kind of thing often, so she gave him a friendly kick on the tush and sent him on his way. She went back to the pub for lock-up.

The next time she went down the Dog & Bone, he was there again.

'You been here every night, waiting for me?' she asked.

'What're you drinking?' he said, his Irish accent back in place.

They drank together that night, and she was impressed by the way he kept pace with her, not bad for a nancy-boy prince, and she told him so. Her words were garbled though, by the drink, and the music which flowed over their heads in its taps and its paces. The fiddlers were on form tonight, everyone nodding their heads to the rhythm. Sometimes London was a very Irish place.

'Bit different than Buckingham Palace,' she said.

'Too right,' he replied, sounding vaguely Australian. She didn't miss a thing.

That night they shagged up against a different tree. In fact, after the musicians finished, they escaped out of the smoke into the night air and wandered up the road until they reached Hampstead Heath. The Heath whispered sex at night, and as they walked, she noticed men flit in and out of the trees.

'Don't forget your condoms,' she shouted out to them. 'It's a good life, to be a queer boy,' she said to Charles. 'Endless variety.' He didn't reply. They found a tree, and then they found a patch of grass, and they lay together passionately. Charlie liked sex, it was unproblematic. It was all the other business that went along with it that proved so trying. But she and Prince Charles were avoiding unnecessary complications. He rarely spoke, and when he did, Charlie couldn't make sense of anything he said. So she ignored him and offered her body instead.

During the day, nothing much happened. Charlie went to work. Well, she went to look for work. She had lost her job a couple of years ago now, and hadn't been able to find one since. Every day she went to the job centre. But there was never anything there. There was supposed to be a boom on, but for Charlie it was all a big bust. She rolled smaller and smaller cigarettes, and stole books for a living.

She didn't see Prince Charles for a while. In real life, that is; she did see him on the news, he was always on the news, him and that estranged wife of his. Charlie went to her usual haunts. She saw her usual friends, and spoke of usual things. She knew better than to mention shagging the Prince. Bonking the Man Who Would One Day Be King. Without the wig, and the sideburns, and the glasses, and the hat, he was truly ugly.

And then one day she sat down on a bench in St James's Park. The park was near the palace, but she was there to see the ducks. She had been evicted from her flat and couldn't think what else to do with herself. The bailiffs had taken everything, which was okay since it meant she didn't have anything to carry. She sat for a while, the sun was shining, and she raised her face to it. Then she felt someone sit down beside her.

She looked around. She could smell him. He smelt of greasy hair and leather hat. His black jeans were torn and faded.

'Hi ya,' she said. 'How goes royalty?'

'Fucked if I know,' Prince Charles replied.

'Good,' she said, 'good. Your grasp of the street idiom is improving.'

They sat in companionable silence for a while. Then Prince Charles got up and wandered away, back in the direction of the palace gates. Charlie sat alone. The speeding clouds in the sky slowed their pace.

A Note on Kate Pullinger

Kate Pullinger was born in Canada and moved to London in 1982. Her first book, *Tiny Lies*, a collection of stories, was published in 1988, and was followed by two novels, *When the Monster Dies* and *Where Does Kissing End?* Her most recent novel, *The Last Time I Saw Jane*, was published in 1996. She has also written for film, television and radio, and recently co-wrote the novel based on the film *The Piano* with director Jane Campion. Her work has been widely anthologized and translated. She is currently the Judith E. Wilson Visiting Fellow at Jesus College, Cambridge, and lives in London.